MOTH

FAIRY

MAGIC

A coloring companion
To the children's book
Moth Dust

For my Moth Dust readers

Seeing your costumes, cards, school projects,
and hearing about your love for Flora and the Moth Fairies
has meant all the stars and moon to me.

x

Bridget Beth Collins

ISBN:9798323940387

"The desire of the moth for the star,
Of the night for the morrow,
The devotion to something afar
From the sphere of our sorrow,"
~Shelley

pectral clouds ripped across the sky, and lightning shattered the forest on the night the moths attacked. In the large, looming Nuthatch Estate, shadows crept out of their hidden places in menacing shapes. Little Henry Nuthatch imagined they were reaching for his secret.

Henry's room was a haphazard menagerie of all his forest finds. Cages piled on top of each other were filled with animals who had been injured or abandoned. He quickly set about undoing all of their fasteners, setting them free. The golden cocoon practically glowed in the moonlight. "What's so special about you?" He turned it over and over in his hand.

Henry was going to run to the forest and put the cocoon back in the crevice where he'd found it. Or, better yet, hand it right to the moths and let them carry it off.

But he let curiosity get the better of him.

He held his breath and pulled the ends of the cocoon apart.
The delicate silk tore.
"What in the…" Henry's face lit up at what he saw.
He was so entranced by what he'd found in the cocoon that he did not see the moths swarming on the other side of his window, diving and hitting the glass.

All Henry could remember of that night was the door opening and the entire room becoming so thick with moths that he felt like he was moving through a cloud to get away.

And the spider watched from her window, tears in her eyes, as they fled their estate with no plans to ever return.

oths circle starlight and flutter at flames. They whisper sweet nothings into night flowers lit up by the silver moon. And deep in an ancient forest, still brimming with the old magic the world used to know, they are drawn to the light of a little girl…

 lora *loved* the moths in her forest, flitting about like specks of sunlight on the wing, and she thought their caterpillars could weave magic. "How could anyone hate creatures that dance in the moonlight, and seek the stars, and make silk?" she said.

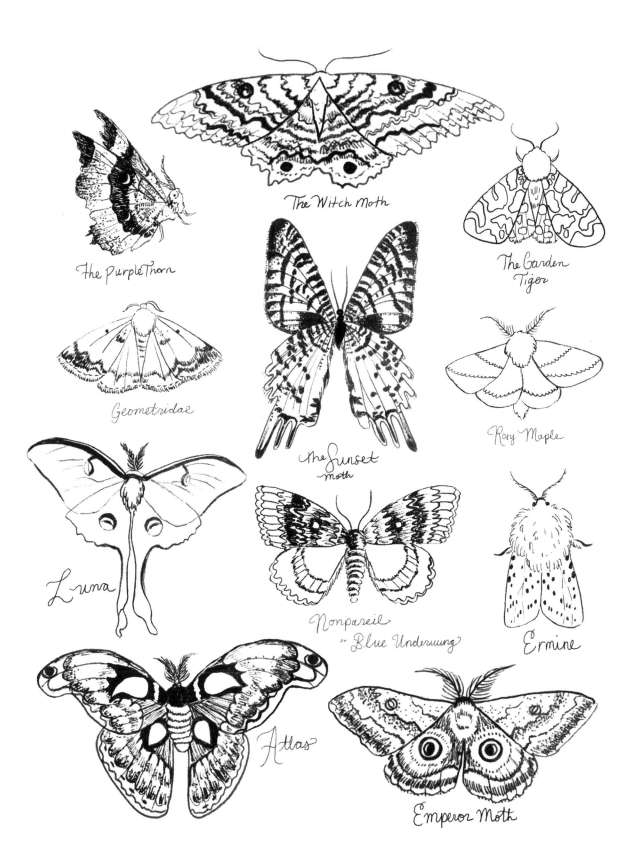

The Witch Moth

The Purple Thorn

The Garden Tiger

Geometridae

the Sunset moth

Rosy Maple

Luna

Nonpareil or Blue Underwing

Ermine

Atlas

Emperor Moth

lora let the caterpillar crawl up onto the tip of her finger. She counted the sections of his body that had orange fur. The woolly bear's orange segments told how many months of winter could be expected each year.

"Woolly bear, orange and black, winter's length is on his back," Flora recited. "Only two!? That will be a short winter. Good. I love an early spring!" She pulled a leather-bound book and a quill from her pocket. The pages in the book were filled with all her vivid drawings and descriptions of the moths and caterpillars she found in Silkwood. There were pressed petals of the flowers they liked to drink from and the little poems she'd made about each moth. She found the page with the Woolly Bear Caterpillar and its orange moth, The Isabella Tiger. She wrote down *1907, two months of winter* in the margin, then she leafed through the pages to look at all her other finds.

he laughed, pretending to do the backstroke through a constellation. The flowers she swam in had tiny shoots poking out of their backs, like the tail of a shooting star. Flora took one and bit off the end of the little tail and drank its nectar. It had the most delicious taste.

"It fills my whole body with light!" she sang. She lay there, drinking from the stars and letting sunlight pour over her as it peeked through the leaves and made patterns like rivulets of water through her closed eyelids. "This must be what magic feels like," she said.

hen the evening air cooled and the sky turned a violet haze of lost sun, Flora swung in her hammock over the stream next to her home. It was a simple stone cottage with a thatched roof and a fat turret that looked like a witch's hat.

lora hung her hammock among strings of brightly colored paper lanterns and looked up into them as moths fluttered in and around them, attracted to their light. Watermelon vines and herby flowers from the vegetable patch nestled around her and brimmed over the stream.

Gran had a fire going in the stones of the creek shore, and a large pot bubbled with water on top of it. She threw the cocoons into the water to soften them, and gently coaxed a shiny strand of silk from each one to pull into her spinning wheel. Each cocoon was made from one long strand of silk that could stretch across the whole forest.

Gran reminded Flora of one of the large fuzzy white silk moths with big owl eye circles on their wings she'd find in the forest.

Flora looked out over the spring where the moonlight kissed it. Flecks of light glistened on the water, flickering on and off in a dance only they knew. Dark leaves from a bower of maple branches nearly brushed the surface, as if asking for a touch of the reflected light. Flora searched the shadows, yearning for a touch of magic just like the branches over the creek. She wished with all her heart that she could be as glimmering and lovely as the light reflected on the water. Oh, to have wings, a sparkling dress, or even a jeweled crown with such beauty. "I love shimmery things," she sighed. "The way the light dances off of the spring, and crystals…and cocoons! I wish I could make a dress just as sparkly."

Gran looked up and stopped her spinning. "Flora, you shine just like those shimmers."

"Beautiful, inside and out. But what really matters is being like one of those geodes in the spring. How you sparkle on the inside."

"You're like a moth attracted to the light," Gran said.

"Why do moths search for light?" Flora asked.

"Because they used to be fairies."

"Gran! Don't be ridiculous."

"It's true!" Gran snorted.

Flora raised her eyebrows, not quite believing, but wanting to.

"The ones in Silkwood were," She nodded.

There is an emerald spot, deep in the forest, where great big maple trees are draped in moss, a stream trickles with glittering mist, and tiny white mushrooms dot their way up trees to where hidden doorways wait."

Flora nestled in closer.

"And through those doors lived creatures with wings as sparkly as the moth wings you love so much."

"Oh! That would be so lovely!"

"They were a regal, powerful race called the Giltiri: The Golden Ones. And they had a special kind of magic that came from the dust on their wings. It made a light that let them weave the most beautiful silken cloth."

Flora bound down the rickety steps of their cottage, led by the scent of toast. She ducked under the dried herbs and flowers strung from the rafters and practically fell into the breakfast nook lined with plush pillows. Gran had just made fresh gooseberry and honey juice and there were blue and speckled hard-boiled quail eggs to peel. Morning light poured in through the stained-glass windows, lighting up the steam rising from Gran's earl gray tea and casting colorful shadows across the table. Everything smelled delicious.

The village of Silkwood was a smorgasbord of cobblestone streets and thatched-roofed buildings. On market day, it was filled with stalls and tents of every color, with peddlers hawking their wares to the crowds. Every twist and turn through the labyrinth of streets brought on new smells that tickled Flora's nose and sights that would make the most stoic of individuals believe in sorcery. Flora would follow the rush and flow of the crowd and peek into stalls to look at wares and chat with shop owners. Her bright, whimsical musings put a grin on everyone's face. Flora whisked past a troupe of dancers jingling with silver bells, ducked under a table covered in mounds of iced confections, and found herself in a brightly colored candy stall.

Gran's carpets and cloth were a kaleidoscope of color and pattern. Flora's world was laced with the sparkling designs her grandmother weaved. Crescent moons, tree branches, delicate flowers in bright colored cloth—each was a detailed constellation of her Gran's artistry. Her weaving was an art so fine and detailed that the townsfolk said her patterns must have been created with some kind of magic.

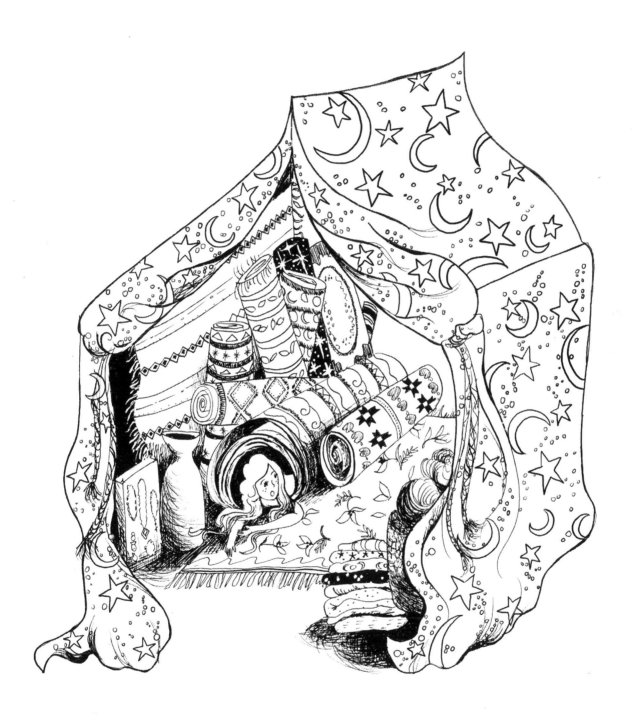

Flora grew sleepy and lay down on the soft carpets. She looked up through the canopy to the stars as her eyes drooped. There was a purplish star there that flashed. Flora tried to see it again, but the branches covered it. She settled in, and just before falling asleep, she saw a black winged creature flutter overhead.

She murmured in a sleepy stupor, "When the large dark wings of the Witch Moth fall, a death or a murder has come to call."

he woman whirled and straightened, her slick silver bun almost touching the ceiling of their tiny cottage. She had high, sharp cheekbones that jutted out beneath violet eyes. Her severe beauty startled Flora, but she found it sticky. It clung like a sweater that didn't fit. A striking necklace with a large amber stone wrapped in silver vines dangled from her neck. The kind with a mosquito or bug inside.

"Oh my dear, sweet girl," she crooned. "My name is Madame Cribellum, and I… I knew your mother." She looked at Flora as though she were a treat she was about to eat.

Flora didn't feel right. For some reason, she didn't trust this woman.

"But it looks as though you're here all alone," Madame Cribellum clicked her tongue and shook her head sadly.

"My grandmother lives here with me. Isn't she right there…?" Flora said, and she rushed over to Gran's pillow and stopped cold. Gran was gone. Flora searched the fluffy bed spread and sheets, but her hopes were dashed… There was nothing but a plump green caterpillar hiding in a little alcove under the pillow.

To find
the light
Look
for the
Mother

*L*et me out!" Flora screamed. The creaky carriage crawled through the night. Flora yanked on the door handle, but it was locked.

Flora knew where they were going when she saw the large smokestack looming toward them, then the large building it was attached to, stretched out like a tarantula hugging the forest.

"The Nuthatch textile mill?" Flora asked.

"Why, yes. It has recently come under new management. I am the head spinner now."

"Didn't moths destroy all the fabric?"

Madame Cribellum snapped her neck toward her. "Don't speak of those wretched creatures!"

he tried to soak up the starlight twinkling down on her, gathering it in her mind like folds of shimmering fabric. As she absorbed the light, the strands in her hands began to glow. It started where her knitting needles were and continued on until all of her creation was almost pulsing with a warm light.

She would find a way out of the mill. She would find a way to the stars if she could! She knitted late into the night, and the caterpillar kept watch.

The next morning, Flora awoke to the light of a pastel-colored sunrise stretching out from the treetops, and long drips of wax hardened across her windowsill. She was snuggled in the curve of her window, wearing the fruits of her late-night knitting. It was a fuzzy, golden sweater that reached down to her knees. It was so oval and plush that it looked like she was wearing a cocoon. Flora felt the soft patterns she'd created with starlight. Moons, flowers, vines—all the memories she had from the forest.

"I won't take it off until I fly away from this place," she promised.

aughing amber eyes stared back at her. It was the boy with auburn hair! Up close she could see the splotch of freckles on the bridge of his nose and the dimples in his chiseled cheeks. He was grinning ear to ear.

"Not your favorite?" He asked.

Flora felt suddenly mute. This boy…he looked like a crumpled-up autumn leaf. She could almost feel the crisp air and smell the apple woodsmoke of fall just looking at him. Even his brown fair-isle sweater reminded her of the cozy warmth of sitting by the fire and drinking hot spiced tea. He cocked his head in a questioning manner.

"His name is Thorn," Ermine said. She nudged Flora and raised an eyebrow. Flora felt herself flush.

I n the middle of a dark, sweltering room, where big machines whirred and cotton dust fluffed through the air, Flora secretly embroidered stars.

Madame Cribellum angled her body around Flora and stuck her nose in her face. "What do you think you're doing?" She yanked the needle and thread out of Flora's hand.

"Making stars," Flora said in a small voice.

Madame Cribellum stared at her. "Excuse me?"

"To give some light," Flora said. She scrunched her face up, anticipating Madame Cribellum's anger.

Madame Cribellum yelled in her face, "RUINED! A whole ream destroyed by your ugly little marks!"

have something for you, Maple!" She grabbed her hand and put a perfect silk ribbon rose inside it.

Maple's eyes went wide. "It's PINK! Oh Flora! How did you…?"

"I used the beets from dinner for the dye!"

"It's beautiful!" Maple held the rose to her face, and her rosy cheeks radiated with glee.

Madame Cribellum seethed. "I HATE PINK!"

Then Madame Cribellum's eyes squinted, and she took out her sewing scissors. She spread the ribbon flower with her long, spindly fingers. Then she held the flower up high, and all the children held their breath. Maple let out a tiny, strangled squeak as Madame Cribellum snipped the flower in half.

Maple had turned a particularly bright shade of rose. Madame Cribellum looked down at her and blinked. Maple puffed out her cheeks and stuck out her bottom lip. Her eyes gleamed in what was one of the cutest little pouts. *Nobody could resist that face*, Flora thought.

There were various makeup bottles and tubes and a large jar filled with a shimmery powder. Flora dipped her fingers into its soft contents and sparkles stuck to her skin. She rubbed them onto her palm. They reminded her of something. Something from the forest, but she couldn't think of what.

Madame Cribellum sighed heavily and grabbed a large makeup brush. She dipped it into the jar of sparkly powder and brushed it across her face. Her haggard face seemed to pull taut at the dust's touch. She flicked more dust onto the top of her head. Then she rubbed it into her skin and hair, and it seemed to absorb into the follicles and pores. She closed her eyes and relaxed. When she opened her eyes, she grinned at her reflection. She batted her eyes and looked up at Henry's portrait on the wall.

"Everything I've done has been for you, my love. Why couldn't you see that?"

For some reason, Flora's nose chose that moment to tickle. All the powder Madame Cribellum had brushed into the air found its way to her nostrils. She felt a strong desire to sneeze, and she twitched. She pinched her nose and looked at Thorn with watery eyes. He looked back in helpless fright, shaking his head.

horn pulled something out from behind his back. "Snagged you one."

"A cream puff!" She held it as if it were the dearest thing she'd ever received.

"You've no idea how long I've been wanting to try one!" She closed her eyes, and then, as if making a wish…she took a bite. It was a dream. Puffy pastry on the outside and sweet cream on the inside. And it was drizzled with chocolate icing sprinkled with pearlescent little orbs.

"Nonpareils!" She squealed.

The children stepped into a room made entirely of glass. It towered above them into a round pinnacle, panes of glass held together with a skeleton of iron. Flora felt like she was under a large cake plate. And growing all along the path that guided them through the room were plants. Some were familiar to Flora, ones she had grown to know well from her forest. Others were exotic. Giant leaves larger than herself plumed out of spiny trunks, spindly vines crawled up the walls, and flowers draped over the walkway. Tall palms and tree ferns reached up and splayed close to the glass. The air was thick and warm.

Flora was entranced. She looked at Thorn with excited eyes.

"Thought you'd like it," Thorn smirked.

"They're Henry Nuthatch's. Remember the article in Cribellum's office saying that after his parents went into ruin, he became obsessed with moths. He must have collected them and made this conservatory to study them. It looks like he ended up liking them."

"It's a butterfly house!" Flora exclaimed. "Only better. Moths are so much more magical. A moth house!"

hey entered onto a tight spiral staircase made of white alabaster.

"It's like the inside of a moonsnail!" Flora said. It rose up into a small room with low walls with tiny round windows. They were inside one of the sloped roofs of the estate. There was a desk made of dark mahogany wood covered in papers, paints, brushes and pens. A detailed aqua and green globe gleamed on a golden stand. There were a couple of plush leather chairs, and lined against the low walls were bookshelves covered in what looked like a world traveler's hoard. Taxidermy, jars of scientific-looking specimens, exotic art, photographs of distant places…

ome on, come on! I have a surprise for you!" Flora held onto Maple and Ermine's hands as Ermine reluctantly went up the stairs, and Maple walked on her tiptoes in excitement.

Flora opened the door to the conservatory and pushed her two friends in. She led them down the path, with a few grunts and nervous whimpers from the girls, and into a clearing directly under the finial top. "Ok, open them!"

The girls gasped.

Flora took the girls hands and leaned in. "Hey, I think we should make this place into our own secret hide-out.

"We'll get in so much trouble if Madame Cribellum finds out," Ermine said, pulling away some cobwebs from a shelf. "I don't need to remind you of…is that an ermine?" She reached out and pet the fluffy tail of the little white taxidermied beast. It was the creature the fuzzy ermine moth was named for. It looked so real, as though it might crawl up her arm. She suppressed a smile.

"And look at this!" Flora handed Ermine a dusty leather tome with a golden figure with a tutu on the cover.

"A book on ballet!" Ermine squealed as she began leafing through the pages of detailed movements and intricate dance costumes.

"And there's lots on exploration!" Thorn spun a globe nestled near a stack of maps.

Maple was finding her own gems. "This book is filled with paintings of iced cakes! They're *dripping* with chocolates. I'm drooling just looking at the pictures! Con…fect…What does this say, Ermine?"

"Confections," Ermine said. She furrowed her brow. "It wouldn't hurt to use this place to help Maple learn to read better…"

"That's a wonderful idea!" Flora squealed. "So we can keep it?"

Ermine put her hands on her hips. "Fine."

"Oh, thank you! Thank you!" Maple and Flora chimed.

"But we have to be careful!" Ermine said grimly.

hen Flora and Maple snuck down to the kitchen, Maple beaming her blush as brightly as she could, the boisterous, plump chef was beside himself and only too happy to give them something other than gruel or boring root vegetables. His poofy chef's hat teetered with delight as he rummaged through the crockery.

"Don't tell your mistress," he said. "She would be furious with me if she knew."

Not only did he give them a pot and some sugar, he let them have four teacups rimmed with gold and painted with flowers.

"Thank you so much!" Maple squeaked and blew him a kiss. They left him sitting among his copper pots, smiling and waving with bright pink cheeks. Maple's charms had worked their magic.

"Look what we have!" Maple brandished the teacups.

"Those are darling!" Ermine grabbed a light green one with white polka dots. "I want the one with spots!"

"You and spots…" Thorn said, rolling his eyes.

"I get the one with pink roses!" Maple squealed.

That left one with sprays of blue poppies and one covered in golden filigree.

"Here, take this one. It matches your eyes." Thorn handed Flora the one with blue poppies. Flora took it shyly, then turned away so he couldn't see her smile.

lora turned the page of Henry's journal, and she was shocked to find a drawing that made her spit her hot chocolate back into its blue poppy cup.

"Hey everyone, look at this!"

The others came to her side and stared in astonishment. It was a picture of a ripped open-cocoon in a little boy's hands. Inside lay a tiny girl with green wings.

"A fairy!" Ermine whispered.

"With pink hair!" Maple gasped.

"Those are luna moth wings," Flora pointed. "This must be what Henry Nuthatch did to make the moths attack! He stole one of their cocoons! And it wasn't just moths—it was moth *fairies*!"

I ripped the cocoon open all the way, and there was a tiny girl snuggled up inside! The cocoon had been wrapped around her like a blanket. She had hair the color of an old French rose and light brown skin. And from her back unfurled the softest, pale green wings with two tiny pink gibbous moons. Their ribbony ends faded to pink, and were wrapped around her feet. She sleepily turned over and winked up at me with her bright emerald eyes. She shimmered with faint light; all the dust on her wings, and skin, and hair glimmered up at me. I had never seen anything so beautiful. Of all the treasures I'd found in the forest, this was by far the best.

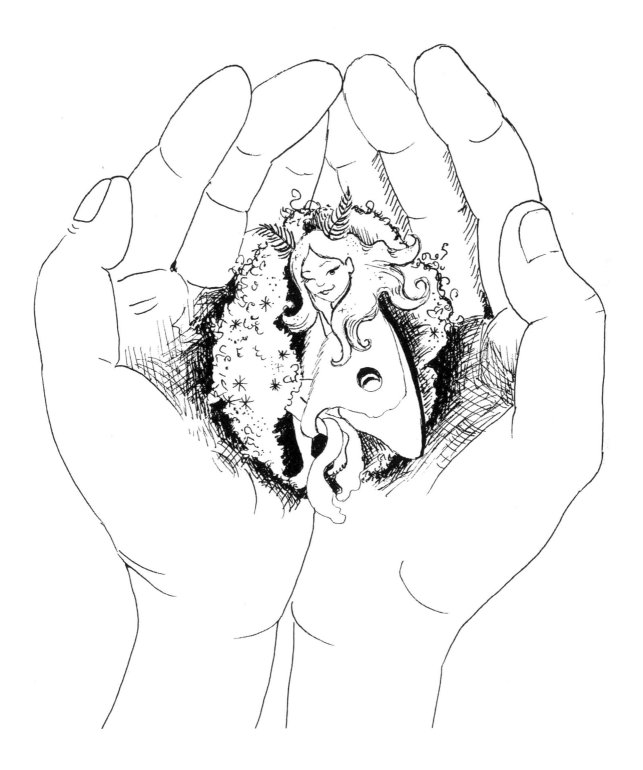

But years have passed, and I had forgotten what I saw—until I saw her again. I was in my garden when I saw her in the sunlight on the edge of the forest. She was picking blackberries. She was human-size, and much older, but I recognized her. Her long rose hair, her thick lashes, and that luminous, almost glowing skin—like a Tahitian pearl. I wondered why she was so familiar... Like a fool I picked a handful of garden flowers and walked toward her.

"I was wondering when you'd come back," she said without looking at me.

"You...you were?"

She turned and smiled with those emerald eyes. Then I knew it was her, for sure.

Lora threw the pool of light into the air, and it splashed up into a thousand little pricks suspended in mid-air. The room looked like it was filled with blue fireflies. The children gasped and clapped with delight.

rmine pulled out a tiny ball of iridescent white silk. She held it out for them to see, then let her hands fall away from it. The ball stayed in midair. Ermine moved her hands in an arcing, poetic motion and the ball began to unravel. Then she fluttered her fingers, and the string started looping into itself, over and under, in intricate knots. Soon it moved so fast, it was difficult to see its movements at all. In a manner of moments, there was no longer a ball of yarn, but a fully formed ribbon floating as if it were underwater. Ermine grabbed it and said, "I've been practicing."

 *Did that tree just talk to me?* She thought. The tree was changing color, or at least the shape was. Suddenly, she realized it was the shape of a boy! Thorn's messy auburn hair was mixed with leaves, and his face was mottled like bark as he stepped away from the tree toward her. Even his clothes looked like the foliage surrounding him.

"Ummm…" Flora looked at him in shock. "Did you just change color?"

"Maybe."

So Thorn *did* have magic. Some kind of camouflage! He was like the Purple Thorn Moth, disguised like a leaf.

he children worked late into the early morning, drying, pressing, and packaging their fabric. Ermine even swirled some embroidery into some of the reams, and Flora used her light to make it shiny. Stars, trees, vines, and even a few little creatures sprawled over their canvas of silken cloth.

Maple would walk between the drying folds of fabric and touch them with her fingers… to her delight, the color would brighten just like her blush as she passed.

Thorn whispered to Flora, "I bet I could make some of these cloaks of invisibility, but that might be a little too much."

Flora gaped. Then she smirked. "We'll have to save that for another time!" She whispered.

Flora's nerves tickled as she put the fabric into boxes and tied them with velvet ribbon. She hoped Madame Cribellum wouldn't peek inside.

 large white silk moth slowly bit its way out of the cocoon. It had a luminous furred body and feathery antennae. Flora sat up sleepily and patiently let it crawl onto her finger. She held it up to the starlight so she could watch it slowly grow in strength. Its soft wings shuddered as it pumped the blood that would enlarge them. When the moth lifted its wings, it revealed two large pink rings circling black spots on its underwings, like the eyes of an owl.

Flora smiled. It reminded her of her grandmother, with her round glasses and wispy hair. And its plump, fluffy body was like Gran's hunchback. It even had speckles like Gran's freckles!

"You glitter the way Gran once did," Flora whispered. She gently touched its soft head. "Are you looking for light little one?"

The moth looked up at her and said, "No. I've found it!"

lora had never seen such delicate, detailed, lovely dresses in all her life. And their jewels! They were dripping with sparkly bright colors. Pearls, rubies, diamonds! They looked like flowers covered in dew drops. One of the ladies had on a pair of satin slippers drizzled in swirls of golden string and accented with big fabric pom-poms. The other had a hat with enormous plumes of silk flowers. They were like the rose Flora had made! She was in awe of their intricate folds and shiny petals and leaves. The ladies tilted bored heads toward Flora.

"Your dresses!" Flora squealed. "Your shoes! Your hat! Oh I could look at you for forever and never need to see the stars or flowers again!"

he girls screamed as something broke off from the crystal ceiling and dropped down right in front of them. It had a human shape and was covered in a layer of dark crystalline crust. It moved swiftly toward them, growling. The girls jumped back. The creature shook out his head of purple crystal hair. Before their eyes, it morphed into…

"Thorn!" Ermine gasped.

"You piece of gum!" Maple stomped her foot.

Flora laughed, "I nearly forgot about your camouflage!"

Thorn raised his eyebrows and sauntered up to them. He looked like someone had gotten him wet and dipped him in purple sugar. He sparkled all over, just like the cavern walls.

 Strung from dangling stalactites was a giant, looming web. Its strands were the thickness of their fingers, and it glistened iridescent hues. In the web countless large wings were stuck.

"They're giant moth wings!" Flora cried. She ran up to the web and touched a large, shimmery one. It was almost as big as she was, and had brilliant silvery dust and fur on its edges, the size of down feathers. "Look how big their dust crystals are!" Flora touched the wing, and a handful of small crystals came off and into her hand.

lora pulled a wing off the web. "I have an idea! Grab these wings with me. I think we could make a big crystal with them!"

Between the four of them, they managed to dismantle and carry all the wings. Sparkling powder and chunks of crystal dropped in their wake.

"Quick!" Flora rushed to one of the vats and shook a wing over it. Glittering scales dropped into the bubbling water. "Scrape the dust off into here!"

adame Cribellum threw back her cloak, and giant Witch Moth wings fluttered up and out. The silvery lines matched her hair, and the purple chevrons matched her eyes.

Madame Cribellum pointed with her long finger. "Yes, Flora. I am the Sorcier Noir. It was I who flew in through your window the night your grandmother disappeared!"

"But I thought you cared for Henry!" Flora said, desperation clawing at her. "How could you harm him? I thought you said he was close to your heart!"

"He is!" Madame Cribellum held up her amber necklace so Flora could see it clearly. "He'll stay right by my heart forever!" Inside the amber, trapped in its frozen golden liquid, were two figures shrunk down to the size of mosquitoes. A man with dark hair and glasses locked in an embrace with a woman with long pink hair and tattered green wings. Luna.

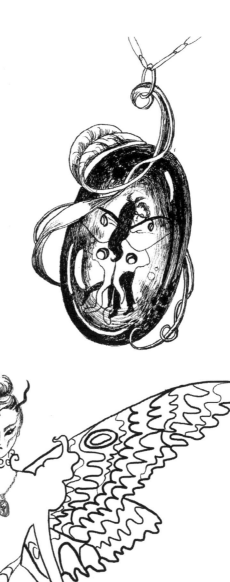

OW!" Thorn yelled.

The children let the fabric on the crystal fall to the windowsill, and the orange sun bathed the crystal with light. It refracted it like a prism, and hundreds of rainbows filled the room. A searing beam of light shot out from the crystal, hitting Madame Cribellum. She flung back against the wall and screamed.

The light pulsated and the smell of singed hair filled the room as steam curled off Madame Cribellum's throbbing body. Hairy black legs began to grow out of her waist, and her eyes multiplied. Her wings withered.

"It's working!" shouted Thorn.

The crystal seemed to suddenly get larger. The window was twice its size and growing still!

"She's shrinking us!" Flora cried.

But their size was not the only thing changing. Flora was astonished to find that the other three now had *wings*!

 flash of iridescent light burst toward them from above. Silver and gold stars on a current of dark gray flooded their vision. Flora's fabric, the children used to cover the crystal, came bursting out of the window in a flurry of sparks and jerked to a stop in midair under the children.

"What the..?" Thorn exclaimed.

"My star fabric!" Flora was shocked. "It's flying!"

"How?" Maple asked.

"There's no time to worry about that now!" Ermine said. "Get on!" Ermine jumped onto the shimmering thing. Flora and Thorn jumped on, too, as some spiders lunged at them and missed, falling to the ground below.

"Come on, Maple!" Ermine screeched. "Jump!"

he clovers were like a blanket of knee-deep snow to them. They collapsed in relief, alighting on the leaves like a feather bed.

Both girls exclaimed, "We're fairies!"

"Your wings are beautiful!" Maple said.

"And yours are adorable!" Ermine rushed to her and touched them.

Maple's wings were pink and yellow, and fuzzy as a bumblebee. Two fat yellow antennae sprouted from her curls. Just as Flora predicted, she was a Rosy Maple Moth. She squealed with glee at the sight of herself.

Ermine's wings were white with black spots, just like an Ermine moth. At their base and between her shoulders, a thick layer of fluffy white fur grew. With her ermine collar and her fuzzy white wings, she looked like she was wearing a fashionable fur coat. She spun elegantly, touching her svelte black antennae. Ermine was finally able to focus on her new wings. She gently touched the white fur along her shoulders and smiled at the dotted pattern that matched all her clothes. She touched one of the spots and lifted a finger to find black matte crystals there. Dust.

"I knew you were Giltiri! And look at you all. Your wings are the exact ones I predicted!" Flora said. She felt proud and delighted. She made them each spin around so she could inspect them.

ventually they rounded a corner of large roots and crested a bramble-covered hill just above the meadow. They looked out over it in astonishment.

"This is a meadow?!" Thorn asked. It was enormous. The weeping cherry tree stood at the other end like a lady with long, flowing hair. But now it was miles and miles away because of their small size. The spring that flowed out of the tree and glittered through the meadow was no longer a creek; it was a raging torrent rushing and splashing over rocks as big as boulders. Every flower looked like some giant confection or decoration of crepe.

"It's like a whole forest inside the forest!" Flora cried.

know! Maple, I bet you'll feel better if you drink nectar from one of the star flowers... Here!" She grabbed a leaf and cupped it in her hands. "Thorn, can you help me? Pull on the stem." Thorn climbed up one of the giant stems and pulled down a flower as big as herself. Pollen sprinkled onto her hair and stamens brushed her cheek. She grasped the tail of the flower and ripped a small hole off the end. Globs of sugary syrup poured out into the leaf she held.

Maple tried to drink, though her mouth was dry and her strength was so low she could barely lift her head. She sputtered, and it seemed like more of the liquid was ending up on her dress than in her mouth, but soon a little color returned to her face. "It tastes like liquid light!"

"Exactly!" Flora jumped up and down. "It must be because these flowers are fed by the stream that comes from the tree!"

hen, out of the middle of the puddle, two bulbous green boulders rose to the surface.

"What are those?" Maple asked. "Rocks?"

"It looks like they're covered with slime," Ermine said, disgusted.

"I don't think those are rocks," Thorn said. "I think they're skin."

Sure enough, black slits opened in the boulders, and the children discovered…

They were eyes.

"It's a bullfrog!" Flora yelped.

The caterpillars fed them outside their den at a mushroom table. They were each given a salad in an acorn cap. They licked their lips savoring every bit of their mint, oregano, and tiny muscari flowers tossed in huckleberry syrup. To drink, they were given rose petals with large dew drops inside.

hey stumbled through a patch of mushrooms, and Ermine suddenly looked ridiculous with a clump of tiny, long white enoki mushrooms popping out of her head. Maple stifled a giggle, only to sprout one large red mushroom with white spots from her own head, like a hat. Flora couldn't help but squeal; it was so adorable.

"Shhh!" Thorn turned to keep her quiet, then let out a snort. Flora had ruffly chanterelle gills flowing through her hair.

"You should see yourself!" She retorted.

He had grown a halo of rainbow fungi out of his head. He flashed her a crooked smile.

horn grabbed one of the cherry blossoms flowing past and pulled himself up into its cup. They could use the flowers as tiny boats! Flora whisked another flower to herself and got in. They looked like they were wearing fluffy pink tutus.

The owl's outer feathers were slick and looked like flecks of ash and sparks on cedar smoke. But underneath, they were soft and white. Flora dug her hands deep into his downy layers and held tight. Twilight twinkled all around them. The moon shone out of a constellation like an iridescent pearl on a strand of diamonds. The wind filled her hair with the vanilla scent of ponderosa pine.

oon, they were under the shattered pink light of the moon through cherry blossoms, like a canopy of delicate stained glass.

"It's beautiful!" Ermine cried.

"So. Much. PINK!" Maple yelled.

A trail of glowing mushrooms grew out of the moss on the bark like steps. They dotted up the tree like a stairway. Thorn bounded from one to another, and the others followed. The mushrooms spiraled up the trunk and jutted out over the water that flowed out of the tree's roots.

 fluffy silk moth with two pink circles on its wings fluttered out of the cherry blossoms and landed next to Flora. It was the Emperor Moth. Maple, Ermine, and Thorn gasped and retreated to the back of the room.

"The caterpillars have lit their tents to welcome their princess," the moth said.

"It's you!" Flora yelped, delighted.

"I'm sorry it took me so long to come to you!" the moth said, "I was luring the spiders in a different direction. But they will soon realize their mistake. We don't have very much time!"

"Who is she?" Ermine asked.

Gran? Is that you?"

"Yes, it's me," the Emperor Moth said, smiling.

aterpillars!" Ermine cried. Spindle had two pine needles in her mouth and presented them to Ermine. To her small size, they were as big as knitting needles. "We can make nets!" Spindle said.

"That's a great idea!" Ermine twirled one of the needles between her fingers. "Let's get to work."

Several more webworms catapulted into the branches, spewing silk, and Ermine quickly took up the ends. Together, she and the webworms began knitting.

It was as if starlight had melted down and shimmered into string. A lacy net of flower patterns and filigree began forming against the darkening sky. Ermine fluttered her wings and pirouetted through the air while using her magic. She flipped and twirled, spinning her threads. A fairy of moon beams made malleable. A sight to behold.

horn sprang up, trying to dart away, but the spider grabbed his leg before he could escape and pushed him down into the rubble. Thorn lay flat, frozen in fear. He was staring up into the underbelly of the beast. It reared up, ready to strike. Thorn squinted his eyes, trying to look away before death came...

Spines hurled into the spider's face as Bear's orange and black hairs exploded out of his body. He was swooping past on a strand of silk. The spider hissed and let Thorn go. Thorn darted, quick as an arrow, into the air.

"Nice shot, Bear!" Thorn called. He yanked one of the spikes from the spider's back to use as a dagger.

"You're not so bad yourself!" Bear said, shooting more spikes into the fleshy behind of another spider, "We seem to be scaring them off!"

here was a loud ripping sound, and slowly, a faint light shone from the hollow where Flora lay.

"Look!" Maple cried.

Flora was glowing.

"What?!" Madame Cribellum cranked her neck to see. "NO!"

Flora opened her eyes and pulled herself up from the bark.

She could feel them, In her heart she had known all along... Her sweater was a cocoon! The silk her grandmother had given her was magic, and she'd whispered her own into it as well. Flora looked over her shoulder. She. Had. WINGS!

They shimmered with rippled lines of silver and gold... just like the sparkles on the water. And each upper wing had a small bright spot in the squiggles, like a star.

She was an underwing moth! Her hind wings were a midnight black with white scalloped edges, and to Flora's delight, each wing had a brilliant blue band, that, when brought together, made a crescent moon. They matched her sapphire eyes! Underneath, her wings were pale moonlight blue with bands of black crescents. She was enfolded in their glow. Her wings were so beautiful, she could barely breathe at the sight of them. She looked like a cerulean night sky.

own from the cherry blossoms, the Giltiri flew. Gathering in the glade, they joined in a circle, transforming back into their true forms. Some were teeny and golden, some large and mottled with wild patterns, some soft and muted. Stripes, spots, and checks, they were a kaleidoscope of color.

he spring vibrated softly. A dim light from under the surface grew stronger and stronger. White foam dispersed to form a circle of aqua water. Then, two figures rose up out of the water, suspended in sparkles.

They lit up, and all could see they were Luna and Henry, restored. Luna's wings were delicate and translucent. They were a pale green, almost aqua. Their long pink tails trailed beneath her like ribbons. And somehow, Henry now had wings too! His upper wings looked like a black and white animal print, like a leopard. His hind wings were orange with black spots. Henry and Luna embraced in the air, just as they had been in the necklace, then slowly awakened.

Henry looked down at her and shook his head in awe. "We're free!" He kissed her gently on the forehead. Then she grabbed his face and kissed him passionately. The crowd cheered as Henry's face blushed. They landed on the shore to a cheering audience.

Luna brushed a finger on Henry's wing and said, "Look what I gave you!"

He opened his wings and examined them. "The Garden Tiger Moth!"

ran introduced Flora to an elderly Giltiri man with long white hair and kaleidoscopic wings. Gran held his arm close and nearly squealed when she told her, "Flora, this is your grandfather, Ripheus!"

"Whaaat?! I never expected to have a grandpa!" Flora held out her hand to shake his. Ripheus seemed to be where Flora got her fiery spirit from, because instead of shaking her hand, he grabbed Flora and spun her around. "My little love!"

"You have Sunset Moth wings!" Flora gasped. They were striking black like her underwings and really did look like a fiery multicolored sunset with bright orange, aqua, and pink.

"Do you like them?" He flashed a proud grin and turned for her to see them in all their glory. "Fit for a king, eh?"

"Don't encourage him," Gran said, rolling her eyes.

iltiri magic had filled the forest again. The sky turned a moody charcoal as the moon settled in the nook of the low sky. Lanterns made of glow worms inside flowers were strung in a glen of soft moss and sparkling dew. A grand feast was prepared of sautéed mushrooms, fiddlehead flatbread, nettle salad, sugared violets, and star flower wine. The smells drifted through the ferns and curled in Flora's nose.

All of the moth fairies came in elaborate silk wear they had retrieved from their old haunts. Their magical couture entranced Flora. There were tiny crystal beads threaded with silver and gold, flowers and vines made from moon-glow ribbon, jewel beetle buttons, hummingbird feather crowns, and all of their glorious wings splayed for the dances. They put the Parisians to shame!

Gran gave Flora a gossamer lace dress to wear that looked like it had been threaded with starlight. And under the skirts, a petticoat of the palest, iridescent blue. "To match your wings, love," she said.

The fairies danced and danced in the glen, smitten through with glowy magic, and where their feet touched the ground… a fairy ring of mushrooms grew.

lora stilled and looked up at the glittering sky. She said, "In the end, I realized that nothing can take your light. Nothing can steal it. You can't use it up, and it can't ever run out. And once you let go of your fear... let yourself enter the darkness with the knowledge that not even death can snuff it out... Then you are free to shine."

Thorn sidled up to Flora as they soared over the forest, and he put his hand out for her. She smiled back at him and put her hand in his.

"Your wings are as bright as you are," he said, and kissed her on the cheek.

The moths had finally found their light.

f you are looking to thread starlight into one of your gowns, embellish forest fronds onto a new hat, or have slippers that shimmer like a babbling brook, there is a special place for you to peruse. There is a fabric shop in a tiny town near the forest's edge. It has the most luxurious, smooth silk covered with delicate designs. There are four shop owners who dress as beautifully as their fabric.

The head weaver wears thick white furs, black dotted Swiss gowns, and intricate braids in her hair. The bookkeeper wears brown herringbone and tweed suits with a pheasant-feathered hat. The fashion designer is a profusion of pink, with silk roses dotting her dresses and sometimes a touch of yellow to match her wavy bob. The embroiderer wears shimmery lace with secret blue petticoats hidden beneath her skirts… to match her sapphire eyes. The four seem so happy together; it is almost as unbelievable as their wares. People come from far and wide to buy their fabric and are always delighted by how wonderful their new cloak, carpet, or dress makes them feel.

"Like magic!" they say.

And it is.

ABOUT THE AUTHOR

Bridget Beth Collins lives in Seattle with her husband and three boys. She grew up playing barefoot in the wild forests, gray sand beaches, and frothy gardens of the Pacific Northwest. She follows whatever creative whim strikes her fancy and shares it as Flora Forager online. Some of her favorite things are spicy herbal tea, meandering walks with her dog, getting crushes on flowers, and imagining herself in a magical world.

Books:

Moth Dust
The Art of Flora Forager
Flora Forager ABC
The Fairy Journals
Flora Forager: A Seasonal Journal Collected From Nature
Metamorphosis: A Flora Forager Journal

Find the QR code in this moth to
easily fly to floraforager.com where you can
find Bridget Beth Collins' paintings,
flower art prints, and more.

Made in the USA
Monee, IL
24 September 2024

66463656R00070